Echoes of the Soul

Poems on Life, Emotions & Beyond

JIYA DHAMA

Prints Publications Pvt Ltd
New Delhi

Published by

Prints Publications Pvt Ltd
Viraj Tower- 4259/3, Ansari Road,
Darya Ganj, New Delhi-110002, India.
Phone : 91-11-45355555
E-mail: contact@printspublications.com

Edition: 2024

ISBN: 978-93-66972-38-1

Published and Printed by Mr. Pranav Gupta (Managing Director) on behalf of Prints Publications Pvt Ltd, New Delhi.

CONTENTS

WOMEN

Independent as an individual
United as a gender
I am a woman
I am a living wonder
Strong on the inside
Although i might seem tender
Black or white
I am splendour
Scared of the society
Pressurised ed by toxic masculinity
Facing unimaginable cruelty
Due to the men in insobriety
Who can be defeated
if i can create a mere trinity
I might seem weak
I might seem easy to over power
But if i stand strong my grounds
Each and every demon i can devour
I can easily blow ur mind
Dear mankind
Don't underestimate my power
U might call urself a pillar
but I am a full fledged tower.

LOSS CAN BE PROFOUND

With every tick of a clock
In every blink of an eye
Notions and opinions we create
As time effortlessly passes by
In all the time we've lost
New memories we've found
Some a little bittersweet
Some extremely profound
For we have a lot to lose
But with loss comes gain
Losing someone or something isn't easy
But with time our memories heal the pain
We've all lost something precious
An article of which memories we hold
Something not of much worth maybe
But in our eyes more valuable than gold
The stick figure drawings we made
The sun in the corner of the paper
which brought us pleasure
To us may now be "kiddish or ugly"
But our parents shall forever cherish it as their treasure
Bandaids don't fix bullet holes
For loss leaves our hearts void
With time we lose things and people
As death is a loss we can't avoid.

THAT GIRL

I will never be the girl
Who will be called pretty
Never shall the adjective beautiful
Be used to describe me
Because I will never be the girl
With a flat stomach
Or a perfect smile
I will never be the girl
With the perfect sense of style
I don't have the perfect body
Thin and dainty arms
I'm not perfectly feminine
Not fragile like pandora charms
I will never have the perfectly round face
I will however always have a crooked smile
The small eyes, the messed up hair
Simply be the girl whose not worth while
I will always question my beauty
For I will always have the scars
I shall never be a pretty girl
But always the girl of ink and stars.

DARKNESS

The darkness we would fear as a kid
Switch off all lights and skid
Today the same darkness
Allows me a minute of peace
A minute of quiet
Where everything isn't overwhelming
My thoughts aren't in a riot
And just like that a dark room
Is no more a punishment but a choice
When everything is toned down
And I can hear my inner voice
From being the sunshine girl
To being a selenophile
The darkness gives me the comfort
A second or two to reconcile.

RELATIONSHIPS

Attraction repulsion
Hate and love
These emotions we hold in our hearts
When relationships we define based on the above
But what is a relationship
An invisible string perhaps?
Perfectly secured to both ends
Too loose or tight and it will collapse
Or are they just based off science
And not actually heartfelt
Gravity doing it's thing,
Like Newtons love towards the apples pelt
Relationships we have
with everyone we know
Some bring us joy
while some end in sorrow
Friends families and significant others
Distant relatives with ones who gained fame
But some truly are complicated relationships
Which we simply cannot name.

JUST A REGULAR NIGHT

Out in the sky
Where the stars shine bright
The moon so extravagant
With its pearly light
Yet in my room
Alone I lie
Staring at the ceiling
Minutes and hours passing by
Drowsiness in my voice
Bags under my eyes
To sleep is a choice
But not to rise.
100 things on my mind
99 of which are worries
The remaining one thought
Crushed and turned to slurry
Finally at 4
Tired and I'm vein
My body gives up
Surrenders itself to pain
And out in the sky
When the stars shine bright
Alone in my room I sigh
On a regular night.

NEW YEARS EVE

On the night of New Year's Eve
Midst all the merry sound
The cheering and the laughing
I quietly sit on the ground
I Take out my phone
Scroll through the pictures
As tears roll down my eyes,
A truly emotional mixture.
Then I hit "play"
On the album named memories
Showcasing the transition
From sunny days to December breeze
There's pictures of parties
Pictures of days we had fun
Pictures of the work I missed out on
Pictures of a lost loved one
So when I go to sleep tonight
The rollercoaster will start again I believe
As I watch alas the moon shine bright
On the night of New Year's Eve.

OH HOW IT WOULD BE

Oh how it would be
If I could capture her beauty
See herself through my eyes
Compare her looks to sunset skies
Oh how it would be
If it wasn't for that guy
She'd still have the confidence
Of her 5 y/o self
Blowing kisses to each and every mirror
She passed by
Oh how it would be
If she could see
How oh how pretty
She seems to me
A pretty face on the outside
Beauty lies within
Possessing both these qualities
Would be her biggest sin
Oh how it would be
Oh me oh my
For her to love herself
Not look into the mirror and sigh.

ARE YOU OKAY?

When I sit in a corner and cry
Sulk the whole damn day
And known people passing by
ask me if I'm okay?
If I was fine, why would I cry
Why would I sulk , shout or scream
Why would I fake saline tears
Why wouldn't I just live the life of my dreams
Realisations dawn
Life takes unexpected turns
And the brave face we have to put on
Under the rage and fear it burns
Sunsets are pretty, perfect and divine
But thunder storms show us that sometimes
nature too needs to scream and shout to be fine.

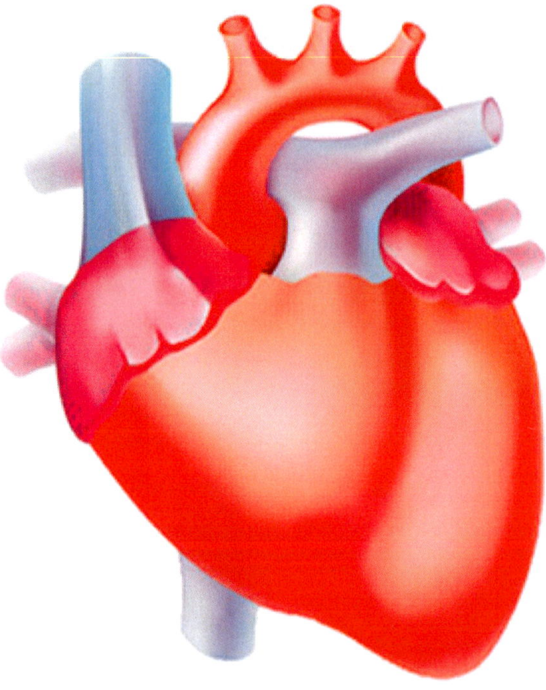

HEART?

A human heart full of arteries and veins
Romantically hurt, it bleeds and pains
Scientifically researched, studied through cardiology
Yet beats faster through confessions and apology
It's funny how small actions of love
Can make it skip a beat
Where debates around the world go on
The heart is where feelings and science meet
The sense of recognition
A box of chocolates with a loving note inside
Makes any human's heart beat faster
Your face with a smile too bright to hide
A complex structure which keeps us alive
It Beats every second
Yet has the power to love a soul
Many other feelings beckoned.

It is NOT okay

It is not okay
Making fun of someone for the sake of entertainment
Making a joke that hurts one's feelings
You do not know what's going on inside their head
You do not know from what past traumas they're still healing
It's not okay.
To apologise for something
And do it all over again
Only to make them feel worse about themselves
And that they are truly the ones to disdain
It is not okay.
To use someone
To make them feel wanted
Then leave them hanging again
Leaving their feelings, their heart distorted
Maybe it seems cool
At the end of the day for you it's fun
But at the end of the day you need to know
Maybe one day, you will be the one.

House in Home

HOUSE OR HOME

4 walls and a roof can make a house
And so could a mansion facing a lake
But what exactly differentiates a house from a home
On that I have a different take
It is not the furniture
The expensive paintings we put up
But what makes a house, a home
Is your Childs drawing on the walls using your makeup
The memories of your loved ones
You being an inquisitive child
To growing up and graduating
Throwing parties and going wild
"Home is where the heart is"
To this, I absolutely agree
But by using this word to describe a place
We often fail to understand and see
How the word 'home' can remind us of a person
Summing up our feelings beautifully.

WORLD

The world is a mess
More of puzzle, a game
Almost as if its chess
We are simple the pawns
Corrupted, we blindly trust
Form strong biased opinions
Which with time we left rust
A world where everyones two faced
Where for the smallest matters, mobs collide
Where the art of betrayal we have aced
Nothing less than a house of horrors ride
"Catastrophe" is really a very small world
To describe the present situations around the world
Where the peace, harmony and environment
are on a constant decline
Where every night before going to bed
I question myself if it was the last day
Of living life just "fine".

HOME

Home sweet home
Where are you?
Why am I living on the street
Where is the shelter above my head
The marble and wood under my feet?
Home sweet home
Oh how I long for you
Four walls and roof to call my own
A little plant or two
And a nameplate to make my identity known
Home sweet home
What a feeling it would be
To return after a long day of work
Snug on the couch
And watch some tv
How I've always wanted a home
But have nothing to my name
As I dream about the soft beds quilts
Wandering if hay and feathers comfort the same.

THE END

Be it the end a beautiful fairytale
Or a painful, hurtful verse
Be it the end of a long drive in luxury
Or the last ride of your life in a hearse
The end is always the beginning
The beginning to something new
Something beyond the concept of finished
Put piece and piece together and sew
"Happy ending. Happily ever afters"
Phrases like above do exist
But endings being depressing and sad
Are myths which still persist
The sky changes shades
Second after an another
Each one prettier, Unique in its own way
So be thankful, for you can see
the end of every day.

BLUE BLOOD

Yeh blazer
Yeh uniform
Bas ek aur saal saath nibhayenge
Phir graduation day pe
Sabko saath rulaayenge
Scribble pe sab inhi ko sign karwaayenge
Bas ek aur saal baaki hai
Phir sab apne apne raaste nikal jaayenge
Dabba ki chocolate aur Fx ki iced tea
White house waale uncle aunty
1-1 ghante tak gate pass na milna
Doston ki pocket faad ke dubaara silna
Paper khatam hone ke baad
Karna khan market ko "hijack"
Stay backs ke baad
Bengali market pe karna attack
In sabhi yaadon ko
Hum Peeche chodd jaayenge
Aur 10-12 saalon mein
Kaheen beth kar yeh kisse daurayenge
Har din yeh laal deewarein
Yeh neeli uniform
Mujhe yeh yaad dilaati hain
Bas ek saal bacha hai saath
Yeh baat mujhe har roz satati hai
Jahan Independence founders mein part leke
Medical room ke gluconD se thakan dur ho jaati hai
Modern, mujhe abhi se teri yaad aati hai.